P9-DMU-762

To Megan Alrutz
for listening to my long, crazy stories

Text and illustrations copyright © 2011 by Mo Willems.
ELEPHANT & PIGGIE is a trademark of The Mo Willems Studio, Inc.

All rights reserved. Published by Hyperion Books for Children, an imprint of Disney Book Group. No part of this book may be reproduced or transmitted in any form or by any means, electronic or mechanical, including photocopying, recording, or by any information storage and retrieval system, without written permission from the publisher. For information address Hyperion Books for Children, 125 West End Avenue, New York, New York 10023.

This book is set in Century 725/Monotype; Grilled Cheese BTN/Fontbros; Typography of Coop, Fink, Neutraface/House Industries

Printed in Malaysia
Reinforced binding

First Edition, February 2011
20 19 18 17 16 15 14 13 12 11
FAC-029191-18222

Library of Congress Cataloging-in-Publication Data on file.
ISBN 978-1-4231-3309-4

Visit www.hyperionbooksforchildren.com and www.pigeonpresents.com

I Broke My Trunk!

By **Mo Willems**

An **ELEPHANT & PIGGIE** Book

Hyperion Books for Children / *New York*
AN IMPRINT OF DISNEY BOOK GROUP

I have not seen
Gerald today.

Why?

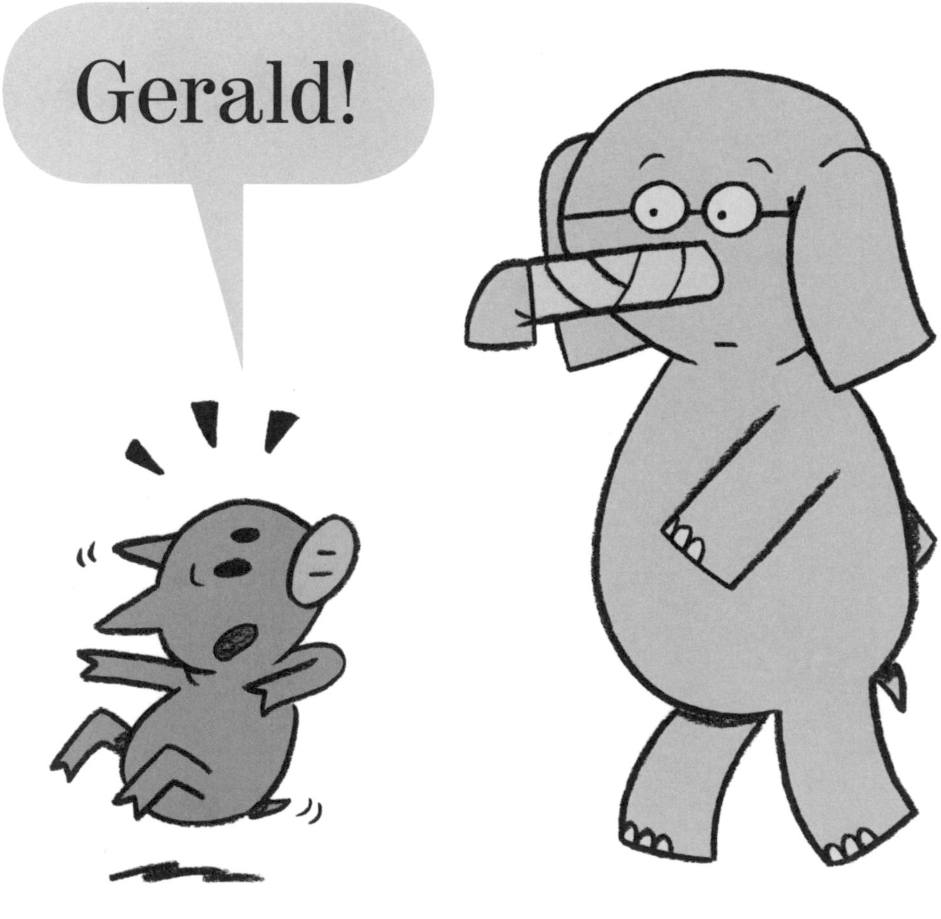
Gerald!

6

Then, I had an idea!
I wanted to lift Hippo
onto my trunk!

13

15

So, I lifted Hippo onto my trunk.

But, a hippo
on your trunk
is heavy.

There is more
to my story.

Rhino wanted a turn.

24

What did
you do?

But, a hippo *and* a rhino on your trunk are very heavy.

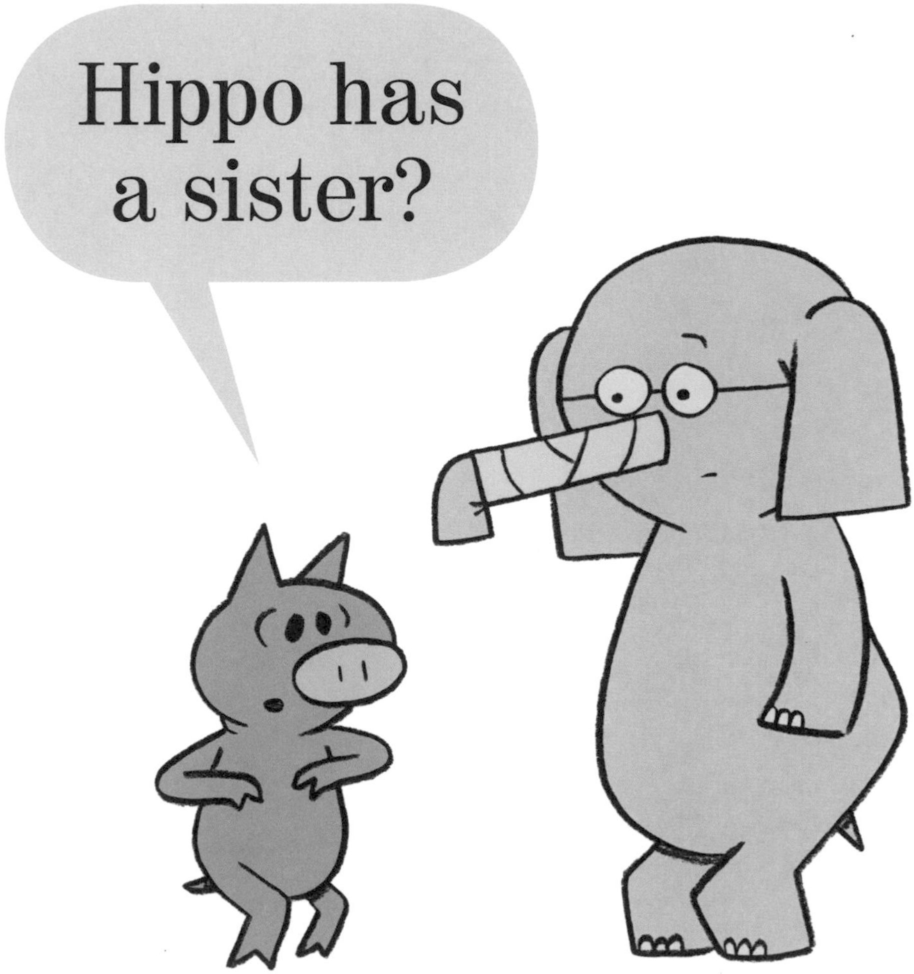
Hippo has
a sister?

36

37

45

But, I tripped and fell . . .

. . . and broke my trunk.

51

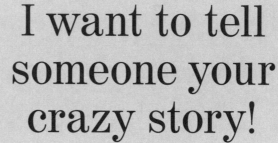

WHOOP!

It is a long,
crazy story. . . .

Have you read all of Elephant and Piggie's funny adventures?

Today I Will Fly!

My Friend Is Sad

I Am Invited to a Party!

There Is a Bird on Your Head!
(Theodor Seuss Geisel Medal)

I Love My New Toy!

I Will Surprise My Friend!

Are You Ready to Play Outside?
(Theodor Seuss Geisel Medal)

Watch Me Throw the Ball!

Elephants Cannot Dance!

Pigs Make Me Sneeze!

I Am Going!

Can I Play Too?

We Are in a Book!
(Theodor Seuss Geisel Honor)

I Broke My Trunk!
(Theodor Seuss Geisel Honor)

Should I Share My Ice Cream?

Happy Pig Day!

Listen to My Trumpet!

Let's Go for a Drive!
(Theodor Seuss Geisel Honor)

A Big Guy Took My Ball!
(Theodor Seuss Geisel Honor)

I'm a Frog!

My New Friend Is So Fun!

Waiting Is Not Easy!
(Theodor Seuss Geisel Honor)

I Will Take a Nap!

I *Really* Like Slop!

The Thank You Book